For my dear boy, Elisha.

Sleep well among the stars.

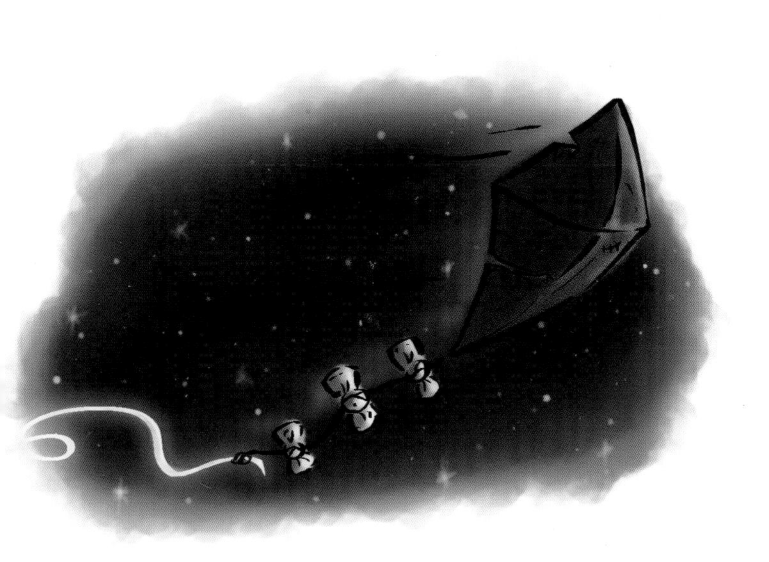

One warm summer night, I was out catching fireflies with my big brother.
We paused for a moment to look at the stars, and he told me some were connected to the other.

He told me about constellations. Certain stars that make an outline, caused by a glowing thread.
"When I was around your age, one was cut, and I had to repair it," he said.

His story took place a long time ago when my big brother
was just a small boy like me.

Even though he was kind and fun to play with, no other kids lived nearby, so his life was quiet and he often felt lonely.

Our mom had noticed my brother was lonesome, so she gave him a stuffed lion to be his bedtime companion.
Even though the toy looked old and battered, my brother came to love him more than anyone could ever imagine.

The very first night my
brother slept with his new
companion, the moon was
sitting just right.

To my brother's surprise,
his stuffed lion let out a roar
and came bursting to life!

The lion was powerful but kind and quickly became my brother's
dearest friend.
Together they found a fantastical world that existed only when the
day had come to its end.

Late one night, a glowing thread drifted in through my brother's window.
"It must've been cut loose from a constellation," my brother whispered to his lion. "Wherever it leads, we should follow."

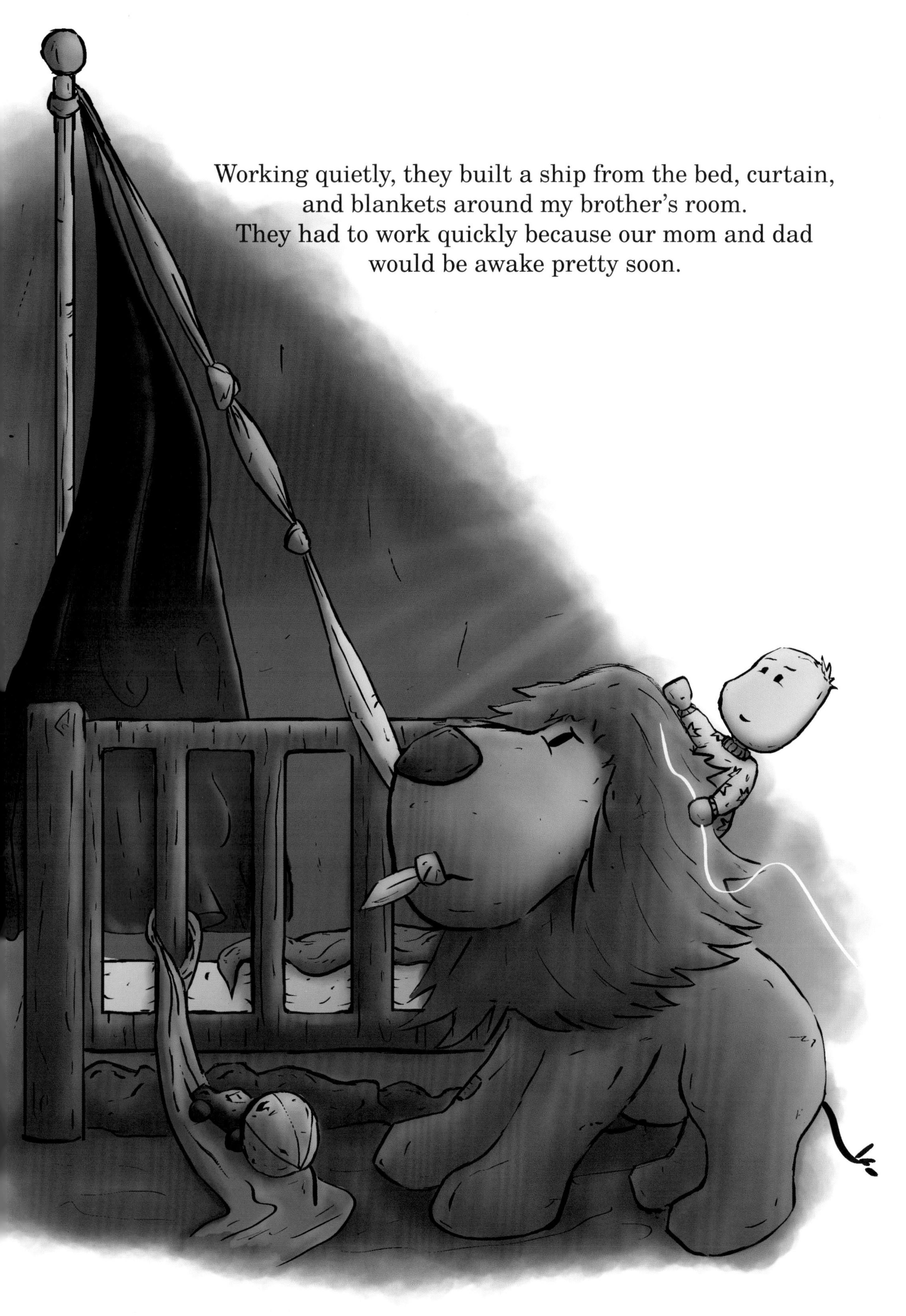

Working quietly, they built a ship from the bed, curtain, and blankets around my brother's room.
They had to work quickly because our mom and dad would be awake pretty soon.

Out the window my brother and
his lion sailed in the direction the
glowing strand led.
All the while being careful not to
snap or tangle the thread.
They sailed past planets, some asteroids and
even a comet in motion.
Far ahead in the distance, they could see the
spot where the thread had been broken

Arriving at the star that had been cut loose
from its constellation,
they'd need to find the thread's anchor, but that
would require some exploration.

First, the search began in a chocolate swamp with
clumps of cream and marshmallows.
They soon happened upon a cookie croc, picking on a
banana man, lost in the chocolate shallows.

After rescuing the banana man from the cookie croc,
he picked up a long golden straw.
He'd been searching the swamp for just the right one,
to play some banana split hoopla.

Later, searching the clouds, they found a mechanical dragon cradled in peaks that pierced the sky. Often the dragon would make a loud hissing noise, and they wanted to find out why.

Turned out the dragon was friendly. He just needed a little help.
A steam valve on his tooth had blown open, causing a loose engine belt.

After that, they searched the hills and found a tree that
grew strange green paper.
For some reason, it was making the animals selfish and
act out with bursts of anger.

They found a new use for it. My brother said it would make sense to me later.
Instead of fighting over who had more of it, the animals used is as toilet paper.

Next, they searched deep in the murky wood and
came across a grumpy Goblin Queen.
Nothing would cheer her up. She was testy and
sometimes a little mean.

They decided to build a stage and put on a very silly play.
The Goblin Queen laughed loudly and all her grumpiness melted away.

Finally, they came to a far green country, where
wild kites soared high.
In the distance they spotted the anchor which
marked its location from the sky.

.mbing the hills, a dangerous
llain jumped out just ahead.
It was Scissorat, the culprit who'd
cut the constellation's thread.

My brother was scared, and a part of him wanted to hide or turn back and run.
But he gathered his courage because he knew Scissorat wouldn't stop here. He'd cut down every constellation, one-by-one.

Leaping high from his perch, the giant rat swung a powerful attack.
My brother's sword splintered with a loud thud and a thwack.

Having no defense, he took a step back but
fell to the ground in dismay.
Suddenly his lion let out a thundering roar,
which made Scissorat scurry away.

The anchor was now clear and with the kite's help, they tied
the line tight.
After a long journey, the constellation was once again fixed,
and all was set right.

They started for home when my brother's lion paused
with some hesitation.
He felt he must stay behind to guard against Scissorat
and keep watch over the constellation.

My big brother started to cry because he was afraid to be alone again.
With all their adventures, he now knew what it meant to have a true best friend.

My brother sank deep into his lion's mane and gave him
one last squeeze so very tight.
His lion purred back at him to let him know everything
would be alright.

By himself, my brother sailed back across the stars and through the Milky Way.
It was a lonely journey home, but he remembered the way.

Arriving home at his bedroom window, he began to realize his heart would never be the same.
Even though my brother missed his lion, he was grateful for their time together and the best of friends that they became.

Many years have passed, and I'm now as old
as my brother was then.
He had finished telling me his story, but I
was still left with some questions.

"Do you ever miss your lion? Is he just too far
away?
Sometimes are you lonely? Can you go back to
find your lion someday?"

My brother looked down at me and then back up at the sky.
With a gentle whisper, he let out his reply.

"No matter where I am, even in places not yet known. My lion watches over me from the stars. I'm never really alone."

The End?